OLYMPIG!

One day, pigs around the world watched a special news flash.

Brent Hamstring here reporting live from the home of a very unusual pig. His name is Boomer, and tomorrow he'll become the first pig ever to compete in the Animal Olympics. Let's talk to some local yokels to learn more about him.

"He always was a weird pig,"
said Farmer Pigbottom.

Terrifically weird!

"I knit his costumes myself!"
said his mama.

"Hold that thought, lady, something's
   coming!" cried Mr. Hamstring.
"It's a bird!
   It's a plane!
   It's . . ."

For Herminio, my hero

PUFFIN BOOKS An imprint of Penguin Random House LLC 375 Hudson Street New York, New York 10014

First published in the United States of America by Dial Books for Young Readers, a division of Penguin Young Readers Group, 2012
Published by Puffin Books, an imprint of Penguin Random House LLC, 2016

Copyright © 2012 by Victoria Jamieson

THE LIBRARY OF CONGRESS HAS CATALOGED THE DIAL BOOKS FOR YOUNG READERS EDITION AS FOLLOWS:
Jamieson, Victoria. Olympig! / Victoria Jamieson. p. cm. Summary: Pursued by Mr. Hamstring, a reporter who is sure he will fail, Boomer becomes
the first pig ever to compete in the Animal Olympics and demonstrates that attitude can be more important than winning.
ISBN 978-0-8037-3536-1 (hardcover) [1. Athletes—Fiction. 2. Olympic games—Fiction. 3. Pigs—Fiction. 4. Reporters and reporting—Fiction. 5. Self-confidence—Fiction.
6. Humorous stories.] I. Title. PZ7.J1568Oly 2012 [E]—dc23 2011015534 Puffin Books ISBN 978-1-101-99779-6 Manufactured in China 10

OLYMPIG!

Victoria Jamieson

PUFFIN BOOKS

Mr. Hamstring sat down to talk with the big pig himself. "The other animals in the Olympics will be faster and stronger than you. Tell me, Boomer, how can you possibly win a gold medal tomorrow?"

"Oh, I'm sure I will win!" said Boomer. "If you practice and try your best, you can do anything!"

Boomer spent the rest of the day practicing as usual.

And he spent the night dreaming of
Olympic glory, as usual.

The sun was bright the next morning, and so were Boomer's spirits. Today, all of his Olympic dreams would come true.

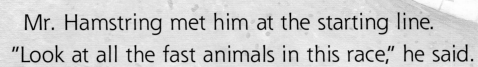

Mr. Hamstring met him at the starting line.
"Look at all the fast animals in this race," he said.
"NOW are you worried about winning?"
"No worries here!" said Boomer.
"Hard work and practice make an Olympic champion!"

Finally, Boomer heard the words he'd been waiting for.

ON YOUR MARK,
GET SET,

Boomer took the loss pretty well.

The cameras zoomed in for a close-up.
"Do you think this was all a big mistake?"
asked Mr. Hamstring.
"A mistake?" sniffed Boomer.

He cheered right up.
"You're right!
This was just a mistake!
I'm sure I will do better
in my next events!"

He did not do better
in his next events.

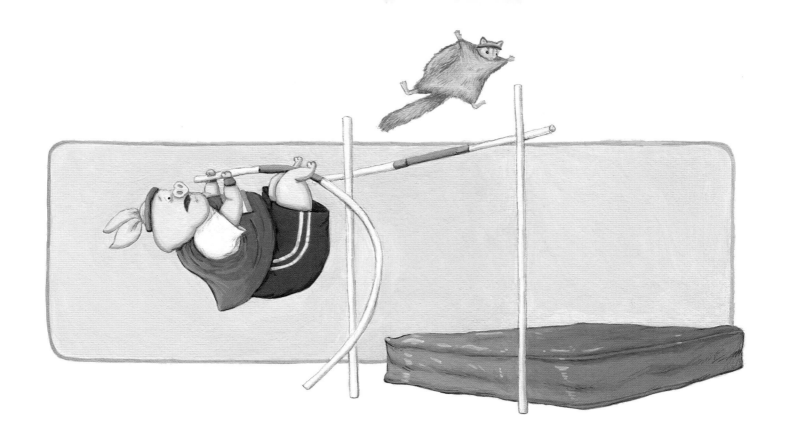

"No mistake this time! Pretty lousy!" said Mr. Hamstring.
Boomer did not understand. He had practiced hard.
He was trying his best. Why did he keep losing?

He lost at hurdles.

He lost at wrestling.

He lost at boxing.

By now, Boomer was battered. He was bruised.
But he knew that he had the very best dive in
the animal kingdom.

One pig.

One pool.

He could do this.

The judges did not like his dive. Boomer did not like his score. He lost it.

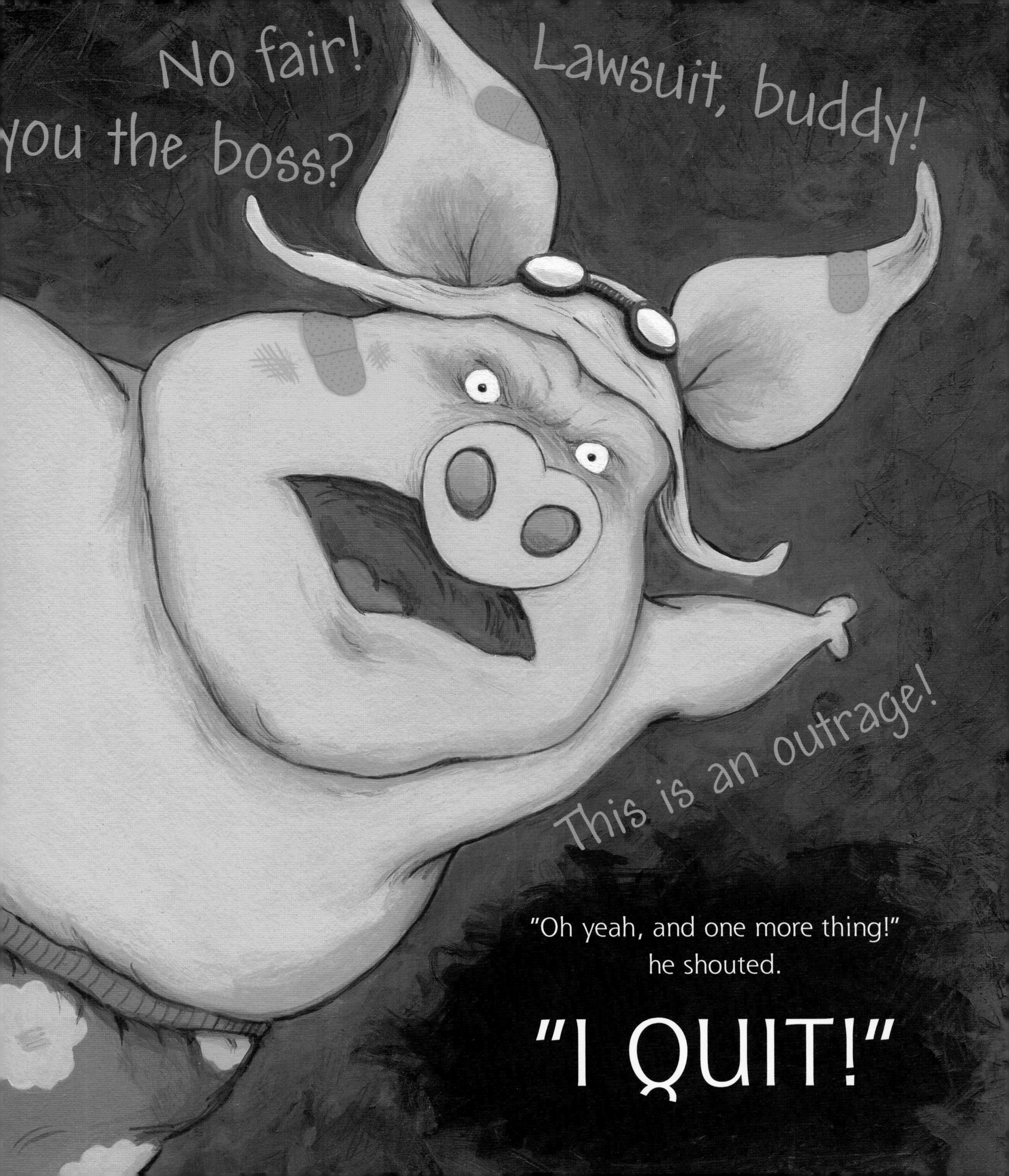

"Oh yeah, and one more thing!"
he shouted.

"I QUIT!"

Boomer burst into the locker room feeling hurt and angry and sad. Some Olympic hero! And soon that rotten Mr. Hamstring would be in to say "I told you so."

But Mr. Hamstring had an even more rotten idea in mind.

There was his mama on national TV! "Mrs. Boomer, your son lost every competition, he threw a temper tantrum, and quit before the final event. Tell me, how do you feel right now?" asked Mr. Hamstring.

Oh, his mama must be so embarrassed by him. So ashamed!

Her voice rang clear around the stadium.
"My son may not be perfect, but he is still my special little
boy! Boomer, wherever you are, I love you and I am so
proud of you!"

Boomer did not feel proud.
Olympic champions did not quit.
They practiced hard, they tried
their best, and they never gave up.
And there was still one event left!

He stepped into the arena. "Ladies and gentlemen,
I am sorry for losing my temper. Without further ado,
I will now perform my routine for the gymnastics
grand finale!"

"But . . . but," spluttered Mr. Hamstring.
"You need a score of two billion out of a possible ten.
    You'll never win!"

Boomer just took his place.

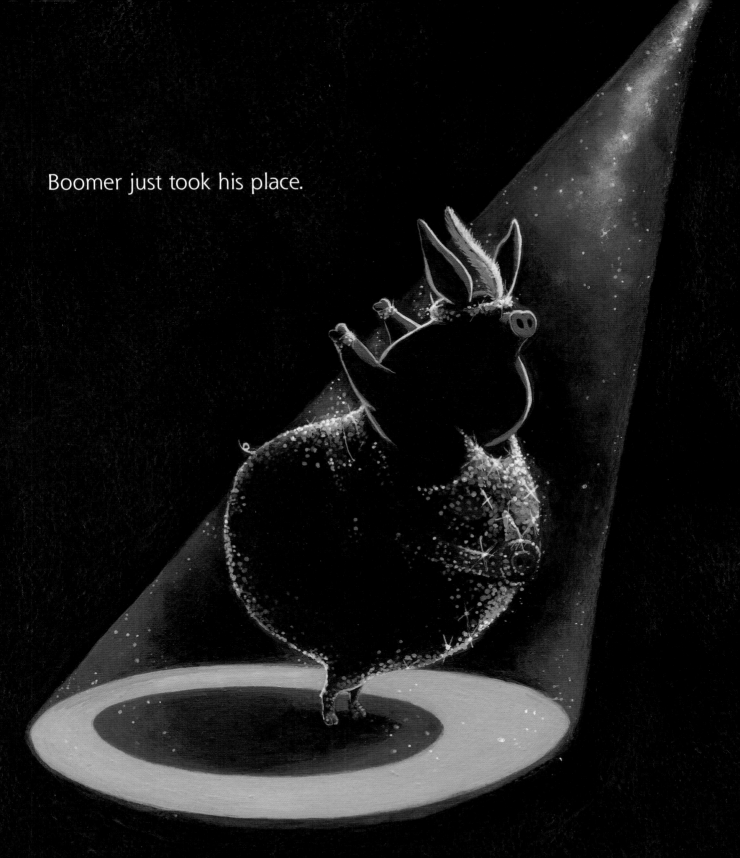

The music started.

He tumbled.

He tangled.

He toppled.

He got the lowest score in Olympic history.
Mr. Hamstring croaked,
"Any final words for our viewers at home?"

"Well, Hammy, maybe I didn't win a gold medal today," said Boomer, "but I realized something very important. I realized . . .